Made possible by a grant from
Fremont Area Community
Foundation

SUPPORTING THE ELDERLY

THROUGH SERVICE LEARNING

MARCIA AMIDON LUSTED

ROSEN
PUBLISHING®

New York

Published in 2015 by The Rosen Publishing Group, Inc.
29 East 21st Street, New York, NY 10010

First Edition

Library of Congress Cataloging-in-Publication Data

Lusted, Marcia Amidon.
Supporting the elderly through service learning/Marcia Amidon Lusted.
     pages cm.—(Service learning for teens)
Includes bibliographical references and index.
ISBN 978-1-4777-7957-6 (library bound)
1. Older people—Services for—United States—Juvenile literature.
2. Service learning—United States—Juvenile literature. I. Title.
HV1461.L87 2015
362.61—dc23

                                                    2014013329

Manufactured in the United States of America

CONTENTS

What was your last school project? Something that involved drawing a map or creating a PowerPoint presentation? For some students, class projects have taken on an entirely new dimension, one that involves reaching out to their communities and helping others. It's something called *service learning*, and for Liz Langley and Ashley Boutwell, there is a great deal of learning that happens in an unexpected place: a local retirement home where they both work closely with the elderly.

"You have to be patient and take things as they come," Ashley says. These words could refer to many different situations, but in this case, she is talking about her interactions with elderly residents she sees almost daily. "They can have bad days, but I love seeing them," she says.

"Don't take it personally," Liz adds. "But they have good stories to tell, and they appreciate you. The longer you work with them, the better you get to know them."

Both Liz and Ashley have discovered that a situation they probably didn't expect to find themselves in—interacting with seniors—has turned into an important learning experience. What starts out as a requirement for a class often turns into the

Developing relationships with older people through service learning can have unexpected rewards.

discovery of a potential career choice, in this case, considering working as a licensed nursing assistant or other job in the medical field. And although both Ashley and Liz are lucky because they have had the chance to spend time with their own grandparents and great-grandparents, for many teens, this kind of interaction isn't possible. And doing a service-learning project with elderly people creates interactions that they otherwise might never experience.

Service learning with the elderly isn't always easy. Like anyone, elderly people have good moods and bad moods, and those suffering from dementia have less control over what they say and do. And the possibility of loss is always there. "My favorite resident passed away," Liz recalls. "He was great to talk to and made me laugh." Ashley adds, "It's difficult when a resident dies and you have to push through the regular routine with the others, even though someone is not there anymore." But despite the difficulties involved in a service-learning project with older people, the rewards are many and they have come to care about their clients. "They like to go out," Ashley comments. "They need more interaction and integration. I'd love to see residents from different units [of the retirement home] get together and have a big event." She has already identified the seeds of yet another service-learning project that could take place.

Is the idea of service learning with the elderly intriguing to you? Many schools now have these kinds of opportunities for students tied into their curriculums. Service learning has become part of almost every school subject and has been extremely successful in getting students out into the community to create new connections.

But just what exactly is service learning? And how can students find opportunities for themselves with rewards that are as satisfying as what Ashley and Liz have discovered?

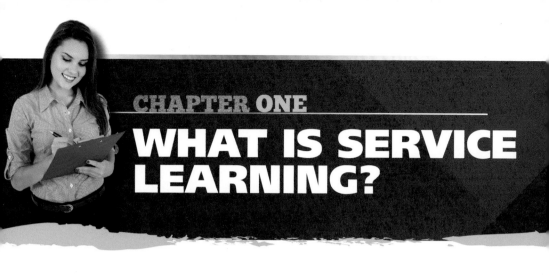

CHAPTER ONE

WHAT IS SERVICE LEARNING?

Maybe you've never heard the term "service learning" before. It might sound like something new, especially if your school or community group is suddenly talking about service-learning programs. But the reality is that service learning is something that has been around for a very long time.

A NEW NAME FOR AN OLD IDEA

There is a Chinese proverb that has been around for so long that no one really knows how old it is or who actually said it: "I hear and I forget. I see and I remember. I do and I understand." This proverb explains some of the reasons why service learning, or simply learning by doing, works so well. This kind of learning, coupled with the benefits of community service, is the basis of service-learning programs. As early as 1916, the educational reformer John Dewey supported the idea of service learning. According to the National Center for Education Statistics:

John Dewey was a famous American educator, philosopher, and author. He was also an early advocate of service learning.

Service-learning has long been viewed as a possible means of improving education, with roots stretching back to late-19th- and early 20th century. For example, John Dewey, an advocate of service-learning, believed that students would learn more effectively and become better citizens if they engaged in service to the community and had this service incorporated into their academic curriculum.

However, it wasn't until the 1970s that the idea of community service really entered most schools. Today, it is common for students at every level, from elementary school through high school, to be encouraged to participate in community service projects. Sometimes it is even a requirement for graduation. It might also be mandatory or even part of a punishment. No matter why it is done, the importance of students contributing to their community has grown every year. According to the National Commission on Service Learning:

For half a century, service-learning has spread in American schools. In increasing numbers, schools have provided service-learning opportunities for students that connect their curriculum studies to activities such as tutoring younger children, adopting a river, creating a museum exhibit, or conducting oral histories with senior citizens. In these and similar instructional activities...they are becoming both better students and better citizens.

But perhaps the best reason for service-learning projects being tied into schools was expressed by General Colin Powell, who was quoted in the National Commission on Service-Learning's article, "Learning in Deed." He said, "Service learning...ties helping others to what [students] are learning in the classroom. In the process, it provides a compelling answer to the perennial question: 'Why do I need to learn this stuff?'"

THE BASICS OF SERVICE LEARNING

Service learning has been a part of education for many years now. So exactly what is it? Service learning is actually a little bit different from regular community service, which consists of meaningful and valuable experience that is usually led by and coordinated by adults and only lasts for a certain period of time. Service learning, however, is actually a learning tool for students. Instead of just showing up to participate in an adult-led project, students who are engaged in service learning actually drive the process themselves. They are given a particular issue, place, or problem to study and learn, and then they have to figure out how to take action in a positive way. While their teacher or other guiding adult will help them, students must do research, make phone calls, and write letters as a way to solve that particular problem. And hopefully they share this community problem-solving experience with their families, friends, and community and can create a real change as a result.

Service learning is more than community service or volunteering. It requires research and problem-solving skills.

Service learning should also be an integral part of the school curriculum and have a clear objective as to what students should learn as a result of their service. It has to address a real community need and involve students in regularly scheduled activities in and out of the classroom. This is what makes service learning different from simply volunteering for community

> ## IT'S GOOD FOR YOU

Service learning might seem like something that students do simply because they have to. But research shows that it also benefits the students themselves. Studies show that high school students who engage in service learning and community engagement score higher on academic tests, develop better problem-solving skills, and have higher attendance rates than students who aren't involved in service learning.

To make sure a service-learning project is going to provide these benefits, students can look for some red flags. A service-learning project should not be any of the following:

- An add-on to an existing class curriculum
- A volunteer experience that only happens once
- Only for high school students
- Only for classes in science or social studies topics
- Only for kids from more affluent communities

service through organizations such as church groups, scouting programs, or other volunteer programs.

HOW DOES SERVICE LEARNING WORK?

According to Learn and Serve America's National Service-Learning Clearinghouse's "K-12 Service-Learning Project Planning Toolkit," a service-learning project consists of five key components: investigation, planning and preparation, action, reflection, and demonstration/ celebration. To get started, teachers and students (this might include one classroom in a school, multiple classrooms, or the entire school) investigate community problems that they might choose to work on. This stage involves research. Then together, the teachers, students, and community members plan what learning and service activities will take place as a way to address the chosen problem. They also think about the administrative elements that will make the project successful. This is followed by the real heart of the project: taking the research and planning and actually doing the service-learning activities. The goal is to create an experience that helps students develop important knowledge, skills, and attitudes, and that also benefits the community by solving a problem. This stage is followed by reflection, when students do activities that help them understand the meaning and connection that has been created by the service-learning project, how it has connected them to their community and society, and what they have learned. Ideally, every one of the five core components should also include assessment and reflection, meaning that students and teachers think about that stage and what they liked or might want to change about it before they move on to the next component. The final stage is demonstrating or celebrating the project, which is often the last experience when students and community members share publicly what they have learned, celebrate what they've accomplished, and look ahead to see what might change or happen in the future.

There are many ways that service learning can benefit a community. Students can choose projects that

Elderly members of the community may benefit the most from service-learning projects because sometimes they are unable to do certain things themselves.

appeal to them and fit with their school curriculum. Different types of service-learning projects might address community health and safety, problems of hunger and homelessness, or working with people with special needs. But one of the most essential and beneficial project areas is helping a population in the community who in some cases can no longer help themselves, and yet at one time were important contributors to their communities: the elderly.

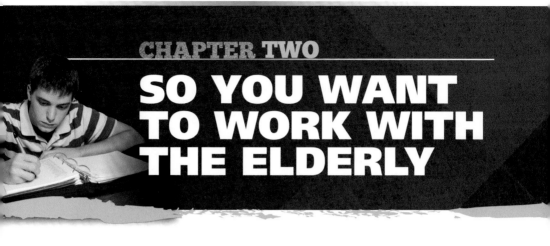

CHAPTER TWO

SO YOU WANT TO WORK WITH THE ELDERLY

The elderly population of the United States is one of the fastest-growing demographics in the United States. According to the Pew Research Center, in the United States the number of seniors is expected to increase from 13.1 percent in 2010 to 21.4 percent in 2050. And as these people get older, they will need more and more help with their daily life, not only with things like health care and rehabilitation, but also with everyday tasks that they are no longer capable of performing on their own. So in terms of service learning, there are many opportunities for teens to work with the elderly in ways that will directly help them.

A CHANCE TO MAKE NEW FRIENDS

Many teens today do not have elderly people in their lives. Perhaps their grandparents have died or live far away. Sometimes families have issues that keep teens from getting to know their grandparents and other

Many teens don't have opportunities to interact with the elderly. Service-learning projects can be a great way to build these kinds of relationships.

elderly relatives well. Or they simply don't live in a community where teens and elderly usually interact. So if a teen is interested in service learning, then it can be a terrific opportunity to get to know elderly people on a day-to-day, personal basis.

Service learning with the elderly can also take place in many different venues. There are things that can be done within the elderly person's home. Other projects might take place through a church or community group. Perhaps a project with the intention of helping the elderly share their own talents and skills might actually take place within a school setting. And some projects will require going to a community center or elderly day care setting, or a nursing home, hospital, or other care facility.

 GRANDFRIENDS

One service-learning project with the elderly, which is popular with younger students (but could be adapted by older students as well) is the idea of creating "grand-friends" with elderly people in their community. They write them letters, send them drawings, visit them in their nursing homes, and sometimes even go with them on outings or help them with small tasks. This gives younger kids the chance to form mutually beneficial relationships with older people, especially when they don't have available grandparents themselves.

However, as with other types of service learning, working with the elderly involves more than just doing odd jobs or helping out at a senior center once a week. For example, rather than offering the elderly neighbor next door a ride to the grocery store once in a while, a teen engaged in a service-learning project might start a community ride-sharing program where elderly people can get transportation to appointments and errands on a regular basis. Rather than raking leaves or doing minor home repairs for people from church once a year, they might create a job bank where students can be available for the elderly whenever they need help. Does an older neighbor want help setting up a new computer or learning how to use e-mail? Rather than stopping by one afternoon to help, students could create a service where they can have technology-savvy teens who can be available by phone or in person, anytime, on a regular basis. Although there are many ways to assist elderly people in daily chores on a random basis, the goal of a service-learning

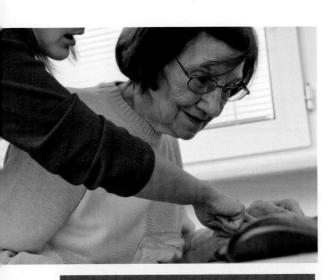

Tech-savvy teens can provide valuable help to the elderly by sharing their computer skills to help them set up new equipment or update their software.

project with the elderly is to create programs that address a certain problem or need, perhaps involving the community through community centers or church groups, and that will hopefully continue into the future even as groups of teens enter high school and then graduate.

ADAPTING THE CORE STEPS

So how do the core steps of a service-learning project work when the target group is the elderly? Investigation is, of course, the first step. Some teens have taken some high school vocational courses in elderly heath care, nursing assistance, or other community topics. They might learn about a need that they see in their own community, such as the lack of transportation for elderly people who can no longer drive and live in a place without public transportation or that is too far from medical services to walk or take a taxi. That would be one form of investigation. They might already have contact with an elderly person or groups of people, perhaps in their own families or through church, and they might talk with these people about what needs they specifically have that might make ideal service projects.

Once they have determined an area where service learning could benefit the elderly near them, the planning and preparation step takes place. This might involve talking with a community center for the elderly, visiting several nursing homes, talking with home health care or hospice providers, and other methods for getting concrete information and outlining a specific plan of action. Teachers and experts in elderly issues can help at this point with creating a plan that is feasible, truly helpful, and sufficiently organized to have lasting value and not just disappear in a few months' time.

Next, the project moves into the action phase. For example, perhaps the project involves determining the need for a job bank of students who are available to assist elderly people whenever necessary. It might take administrative planning to decide how to set up the group and who will manage it, practical planning

Service-learning projects require groups to work together and research how they can best help the elderly in their community before they can create an action plan.

for collecting student information and availability, desktop publishing and advertising to make sure that the target population is aware of the service, and then implementation.

Once the project has been implemented, students will reflect on what they have learned through specific activities. They will think about what knowledge and skills they have gained through their work both in setting up the project and in creating new relationships with the elderly people in their community, and perhaps what they might have done differently or what could be improved, as well as what worked really well.

Finally, there should be some sort of community celebration of the project, perhaps a gathering where

> IT'S TOUGH, BUT WORTH IT

The biggest hardship involved in working on service-learning projects with the elderly is that teens must often accept loss as part of the project. They might work with an elderly person on a regular basis and create a close, personal relationship with him or her, only to lose that person to illness or death. If this happens, it's important to reach out to the teacher or a school counselor for help in dealing with the loss, especially if the relationship has become a close one. Grief and sadness are completely natural. It might seem like something you can handle on your own, but don't hesitate to reach out for support, especially if you have any trouble continuing with the project.

Once you're done, congratulate yourselves! Celebrating a project after it has been completed is an important part of service learning.

the elderly clients come together with the students to enjoy one another's company and talk about the project and what it has accomplished. And hopefully, both the project and the connections it has created will continue on past the celebration point and into the future, either for a certain predetermined scope of time, several years, or indefinitely.

Service-learning projects that involve the elderly might seem difficult or uncomfortable, but they will often help students forge new and rewarding relationships with people that they might never have gotten to know otherwise. And unlike projects that involve the environment or animals or government, they carry with them the satisfaction of knowing that the teens involved have really done something to make life better for a group of people who deserve to be helped.

CHAPTER THREE

HOME SWEET HOME

One of the biggest struggles for people as they get older is their ability to stay in their own homes and still manage the everyday chores, maintenance, and repairs that come along with living independently. Things that once seemed very simple, such as mowing the lawn, fixing a broken light switch, or running to the pharmacy or the grocery store are suddenly much more difficult and sometimes impossible. So when teens are researching potential service-learning projects for the elderly, home is one of the best places to start.

AN INSIDE JOB

Service learning requires thinking through a problem and then creating a solution or plan that can be sustained on a regular basis and over time. So the first step to creating a plan is to think about the specific aspects of what kind of help elderly people might need at home. And the small chores and tasks most vital to everyday life start inside the house.

Even simple, everyday tasks like shopping can become difficult for the elderly, so this is a good place to start when identifying possible service-learning projects.

Start in the kitchen. What might an elderly person need help with? Can they still cook for themselves? If not, it might be necessary to find a way to provide regular meals, or transportation to a place that serves meals to the elderly. Do they need help shopping for food? Shopping leads to other important tasks, such as other errands. Elderly people who can no longer drive themselves and have no other access to transportation might need regular rides to places like pharmacies, other stores, doctors' appointments, and places of business. But these rides need to be available on a regular basis that the elderly can count on, and not have to scramble to arrange at the last moment.

What else happens inside the house? Perhaps assistance is needed with cleaning and small home repairs like changing lightbulbs or tightening a loose faucet that's dripping. Maybe items need to be taken to the attic or brought down from a storage space. It might also be difficult for an elderly person to get around the home safely. Mobility issues might also include removing or taping down small throw rugs and putting away excess furniture or decorations.

A WORD OF WARNING

There are some important points to consider when it comes to doing any tasks for elderly people. Teens, especially those under eighteen, must avoid any situation in which the health and welfare of the elderly person depends too heavily on them. It is fine to set up a regular visiting time with an elderly person, especially because many of them love companionship and conversation, but a teen should never be put in a position of being the only one checking on the welfare of that person. It's too much responsibility for someone that age and could cause legal problems if something happened because a teen was unable to perform a welfare check. Also, it might be fine to help an elderly person by mailing bills or helping organize paperwork, but a teen service-learning helper should never do anything that involves serious legal or financial issues, even if specifically asked. It is also important to always consider not only the safety of the person being helped, but also the health and safety of the teen helper. A student should never be asked to do anything that is physically dangerous, such as climbing up on a roof or doing electrical work, for example. It is vital to always ask for help from a teacher or other adult who is supervising the learning project whenever a situation arises that makes the student feel uncomfortable or unsafe.

MOVING OUTSIDE

There are also many tasks that can be done outside an elderly person's home, again with the goal of keeping the person independent and able to remain at home as long as possible. This can include mowing and weeding lawns, shoveling snow in the winter, taking trash and recycling out for collection, tending flower beds, clearing away brush or other refuse, minor repairs and painting, cleaning gutters, or helping clean out a garage or shed. Stay away, of course, from anything to do with cars, even if you are a licensed driver, because there are insurance and liability issues. Perhaps the elderly person is starting to think about moving out of her home and needs help organizing and running a yard sale. Or he needs assistance with seasonal tasks such as bringing out or putting away summer furniture, or cleaning a porch or patio before the warm season. Washing windows and siding is also a task that needs to be done outside.

Some service-learning projects might involve helping an older person with a task, not just doing it for him.

> A SERIOUS PROBLEM

A teen who spends time with an elderly person in his or her home has to be aware of any signs that elder abuse is taking place. Sometimes elderly people can be physically and mentally abused by family members or caregivers. If teens see any of the following warning signs, they need to report their suspicions to their teacher or supervisor IMMEDIATELY:

- Unexplained bruises, welts, sores, cuts, or abrasions in places they would normally not be expected
- Bruising and other injuries that might be in different stages of healing
- Fractures in different stages of healing
- Cigar and cigarette burns
- Injury that has not been cared for properly
- Injury that is inconsistent with explanation for its cause
- Pain from touching
- Dehydration or malnutrition without illness-related cause
- Lack of personal effects, pleasant living environment, personal items
- Forced isolation
- Repeated time lags between the time of any injury or fall and medical treatment
- Fear
- Non-responsiveness, resignation, ambivalence
- Contradictory statements, unbelievable stories
- Hesitation to talk openly
- Confusion or disorientation

CREATING A PLAN

Once a teen (or group of teens, if this is a classroom project and not just an individual one) has determined what area of home help he or she would like to address as a service-learning project, it's time to make a plan. This doesn't just mean making a list of people on a piece of paper and casually deciding who will go to what house and when. There are many issues to consider: reliability for scheduling, establishing trust between students and the people they will be helping, coming up with a messaging or communication system for both scheduling tasks and keeping track of notes and comments about visits, and deciding who in the group is best suited to performing which kinds of tasks.

Creating an action plan for a service-learning project involves brainstorming and organization by all students in a group.

Obviously, an individual student doing an individual service-learning plan will focus on just one area where he or she feels comfortable and has the most to offer. However, a project involving multiple students and multiple tasks will take a great deal more administrative planning.

Get together and brainstorm: Does one person in the group have a knack for organization? He or she can create a database of students with particular skills and strengths, and collect their contact information and schedules in one place where they can be easily accessed and matched to requests from elderly people.

> ## THE RIGHT TOOLS

Something to consider in a service project that is heavily focused on home maintenance and repair is the question of having tools that are safe and efficient. Think about what a teen worker might have to do, such as lawn mowing or small repairs, and decide what to do if an elderly person either does not have the tools or they are in disrepair. It might be necessary to create some kind of tool bank (and not just someone's dad's workshop!) that service learners are able to access if they need something specific that the homeowner doesn't have.

If the project doesn't already involve a specific group of elderly people, such as those living in a certain neighborhood (for example, a specific community for the elderly) or apartment building, then it might be necessary to spread the word about this service through advertising. Someone who is good with graphic design and desktop publishing can create posters and business cards to post around the community.

It is important to make use of resources. Adults who work in the home health care or hospice fields can offer valuable advice about what is needed, what teens can reasonably expect and be asked to do, and what things are too dangerous or too far beyond the scope of a service-learning project. They might also be valuable in helping identify clients who most need the kinds of services being offered by the project. Community leaders such as religious leaders might also be able to suggest both potential clients and vitally needed tasks. Community service groups like Rotary or Kiwanis might also be helpful in this respect, or perhaps even have their own organizations that could take the service-learning project under their wings and sponsor their activities through the bigger group.

Because physically helping elderly people with tasks in their homes can be a demanding and wide-ranging service, it is probably best suited for a service-learning group for an entire classroom or larger group of teens. Ideally, the project can be arranged in a way that teens passing in and out of their high school years can create a continuous progression of incoming and outgoing workers and administrators. Then the project is more

Some service-learning projects, like helping at a retirement facility, can be maintained over many years if they are well-organized.

likely to survive and not just languish when the founding group of students moves on to college or work.

But what about a student who is interested in helping the elderly but wants to do so on an individual basis, or perhaps does not have enormous amounts of time to use for the project? Several areas offer opportunities for just one teen to make a big difference. And if like most teens, they are tech-savvy, then there are many, many ways they can do seemingly small things that will make a big difference to an elderly person. It's as simple as thinking about the cyber world.

CHAPTER FOUR

CYBER SERVICE LEARNING

Most teens never think twice about using technology in their lives. They use the Internet on their computers, tablets, and phones. They access their homework assignments and grades online, use instant messaging and texting to talk to their friends, e-mail family, post photos, and download music and movies. In addition to user technology, there are also skills like setting up a computer and connecting it to the Internet or Wi-Fi or setting up televisions and media players, all of which take familiarity with components and cables and

Many older people enjoy the latest technology, such as computers and video games, but they might need help setting them up or trouble-shooting when something goes wrong.

connections. All this might seem simple to a teen who has grown up with that technology, but for older people, even these most basic technological skills might seem horribly confusing.

WELCOME TO THE CYBER WORLD

Some elderly adults love technology as much as teens do, and they might be very savvy about navigating the Internet and posting photos online. Some older adults take the other extreme and avoid any type of new technology completely, even when it might enable them to stay in closer touch with their families. Most older people probably fall somewhere in between, and they are willing to use technology but don't know how. They might even have the right equipment, such as a good computer or a scanner, but don't know how to set it up or use it. Others might have once been adept at things like e-mail, but as systems changed, perhaps their hardware or software has become so outdated that it no longer functions correctly, or some glitch prevents them from e-mailing or accessing a web page. Because calling computer and software companies for tech help can be frustrating and even incomprehensible, older computer users might just give up on their technology.

As teens research possible service-learning projects among the elderly, looking at technology services can be a great place to focus. Unlike helping out with home maintenance and daily living tasks, which reoccur and ideally require projects for the long term, helping older people with technology requires less long-term planning. For the most part, a teen might only visit with an elderly person once or twice to help him get set up with his technology and comfortable using it. Then he can return occasionally if a situation arises in which some kind of technical help is needed.

Creating a service-learning project around helping the elderly with technology is also one that can take place in several different types of settings. It could

For older people, learning new skills can also improve their attitude and outlook, whether it is done in a group or one-on-one.

be set up as a series of workshops or programs at a community center where older residents often go. It could take place at a library or church. Cyber service learning could also be done individually, in the homes of the elderly, especially when they need help simply setting up their systems. One service-learning project in Tampa, Florida, involved students actually taking their laptops to a nursing home, where they sat with seniors. According to the mother of one student, who wrote on the From Fear to Facebook blog:

> The [teens] take a computer and they teach elderly people how to e-mail, how to go on the Facebook. How to do the Google Earth and take them into their hometown, and the elderly people are like, "Wow," because they haven't been connected with the technology for a while, so it's exciting for them, and the [student] feels very proud and empowered because they're teaching someone eighty years old and they get to show off their skills.

Service-learning projects that focus on the elderly and technology are especially important as research has shown that more seniors than ever are using social networking.

HARDWARE AND SOFTWARE

There are basically two components to creating a project around the cyber world. One is simply based on equipment: setting up computer systems, hooking them up the Internet or Wi-Fi, and perhaps also connecting a printer or scanner. This setting up might also include installing hardware or downloading programs. The end result should be a system that has the basics for the user to do what she wants to do on her computer, from word processing to e-mailing.

The other component is tutoring. The best computer system in the world, with the most up-to-date software, is only as effective as the user's ability to make it do what he wants. Once an elderly person has his system in place, he might require one-on-one tutoring in specifically how to do certain computer functions. This requires, first of all, knowing exactly what he hopes to gain from computer use. Is he mostly interested in e-mailing family? Sharing photos on Facebook? Downloading movies or music? Once there is a clear idea of the senior's goals, the teen tech tutor can assist him, slowly and simply, in making those things happen. It is important to remember that the tutor needs to keep the technology at a level with which the elderly user is comfortable. Don't install the latest software for lightning-fast media downloads, or a complicated photo-sharing program, if it is too complex and advanced for the user.

Older users might be especially interested in hardware and software for special projects such as family genealogy or history, archiving old family photos, or scanning family memorabilia to preserve and share. This might require a more complicated degree of both hardware and software, as well as tutoring in how

Once they become comfortable with technology, seniors often find they can more easily stay in touch with family.

to save digital images and information both on the computer and remotely, for safekeeping. Desktop publishing programs for creating family history books or photo albums might also be an area of interest for older users.

GETTING STARTED

Helping the elderly with computers and technology is a project with many possibilities and degrees of involvement. If this is a joint project, it might be best to start with an assessment of the technology skills of everyone in the group. Perhaps one teen is a whiz with solving computer problems, while another has lots of experience in teaching his grandmother how to use her e-mail program. It is best to create a database of these skills among the group so that it is easy to match a request with a tutor.

As with any service-learning project plan, it will be necessary to determine when and where the service should take place, if it will be limited to tutoring via classes in a public place, or if it will include home visits and tutoring. Setting up a system in someone's home will probably require an assessment first, either of what the elderly user already has or what she needs to successfully do what she wants to do. It might be helpful to have a professional in informational technology, such as a teacher or a local specialist who might volunteer some occasional time, to help with the assessment. It might be necessary to tailor the system to the financial resources of the older person, and that's where some professional advice can be very helpful.

It might also be helpful to see if there are places where people could trade in technology that is slightly outdated, perhaps after upgrading to a better system. Many people upgrade their computers when they are still perfectly serviceable, especially for simpler tasks such as e-mail and word processing, and this cast-off equipment could be collected and refurbished for use by elderly people who can't or don't want to invest in newer hardware. This could almost be a service-learning project in itself, done in conjunction with recycling facilities or computer technology dealers.

Once the service learner individual or group has defined the project in terms of when, where, and how, it will be time to get the word out. Teens can talk to local elderly care facilities and libraries to set up programs on-site. Advertising materials can be used as well, such as business cards and flyers posted in public places where older people are apt to go, to let them know that this service is available.

A WORD ABOUT SECURITY

No matter where an elderly person is using a computer, it is crucial to talk about computer safety. Sometimes a teen ends up tutoring an older person on computer use on a public computer in a library or other public place as an alternative to purchasing a computer for home. In these cases, it is especially important to stress security. It is vital that the user understands how easily personal information, especially things like online banking, could be accessed without proper use of a password and logging in. Many teens are so used to having their own personal computers that the security issue might not occur to them. On a home computer, talking about virus protection and explaining how hacking occurs might be a good idea as well.

PATIENCE IS A VIRTUE

It is important to keep in mind, when working with older people and technology, that patience is the best approach. Many older people are not only mystified by the technology that young people manipulate almost without thinking about it, but they also feel self-conscious because they don't learn as quickly or remember complicated steps easily. It is also good to be patient with the fears that older people have about technology and computers, or of doing something wrong. According to *The Juggle*, the *Wall Street Journal* blog, "To allay fears, show the seniors that mistakes, such as accidentally minimizing a window or typing in the wrong web address, can be easily corrected. One teen actually took computers apart in front of his elderly trainees so they could see that the parts are sturdy and unlikely to break."

CHAPTER FIVE

A LITTLE SONG, A LITTLE DANCE...

Many teens are actively involved in the arts within their high schools. They might play a musical instrument or sing in a choral group. They might be members of the drama club and participate in plays. They might be dancers who perform ballet, jazz, or modern dance. Or they might be artists who draw, paint, or do crafts. Although many students who are heavily involved in the arts in their schools are used to performing in the theater or during concerts, or having their work displayed in a gallery, they might not realize that the arts are one of the greatest vehicles for service-learning projects with the elderly.

Teens who are already involved in the arts, such as dance, have a good skill to use in developing service-learning projects.

THE ARTS: WHY AND HOW

Why are the arts in particular so valuable to elderly people? According to a resolution produced by those who attended the White House Conference on Aging in 2005, "Research suggests that active participation in the arts and learning promotes physical health, enhances a sense of well being among older Americans, improves quality of life for those who are ill, and reduces the risk factors that lead to the need for long-term care. Participation in arts activities might lead to intergenerational exchange of values and knowledge." A service-learning project in the arts not only promotes

 DEFENDING THEMSELVES

Some of the best service-learning projects can come from unexpected places. Leah Schoen is a seventeen-year-old from New Jersey who has worked her way up through the ranks to earn a black belt in tae kwon do. She decided to take advantage of her martial arts ability and use it to help seniors learn self-defense. She designed an hour-long class to teach elderly people specific moves that they can use to defend themselves and compensate for their reduced physical abilities. How did she get the idea? "I never realized the increased dangers to the elderly until my grandmother had her purse snatched," Leah explained to the *Amarillo Globe-News*. "Watching her reaction and recovery empowered this program."

these factors with older people, but as a student project, it also encourages the exchange between teens and the elderly, too.

When considering a service-learning project with the elderly based on the arts, however, the first decision to make is whether the project will be performance-based or participatory. In other words, will students create and perform with seniors as their audience, or will the project actively involve seniors and allow them to participate in making music, dancing, or creating art alongside the students? This decision might depend in part on the group of seniors to whom the project is targeted. If the project intends to work with seniors in a nursing home who are largely unable to get around well and spend most of their time in chairs or beds, the project will probably be based on performances. However, if the elderly population involved in the project is still healthy and relatively mobile, the project could be

Sharing a love of music can be beneficial to both the service learner and the person she is helping.

based more on participation, especially in physical performances like dancing and theater.

Performance-based projects might include students creating, rehearsing, and putting on plays, musical performances, or dance performances for seniors on a regular basis. Art students might create "gallery" shows of their projects, or decorate the seniors' environments on a regular basis with changing displays of artwork.

Research shows that participating in the arts, such as painting, can benefit the elderly physically and mentally.

Participatory projects can take more planning. One example of a successful participatory service-learning project was done between the Pikesville High School Concert Choir in Maryland and a local senior center. The partnership was created as a way to provide a choral singing activity for seniors that would be meaningful and active. The music director chose music that was appropriate for both high school students and senior citizens, and the two groups practiced independently until they were ready to sing together. Now called the Intergenerational Chorus, this group performs together at both the school and the senior center. They also perform at community concerts and events. This service-learning project allowed students

 **LET'S SING**

Another service-learning idea related to music involves exchanging songs. Students can learn songs from previous eras, as well as sharing some of the songs that they currently sing. They get together with seniors for a sing-along, then the students entertain the elderly by singing their new songs for them. Afterward, seniors and students break into pairs and talk about the meanings behind the older songs, as well as any memories that the seniors have about those songs or the time periods when those songs were popular. And students might find themselves trying to explain modern songs to their older audience!

to actively interact with seniors in a way that benefitted them both and allowed them to share a love of making music.

A WORD OF CAUTION

Interactive arts projects, especially those that involve a degree of exercise like dance or even drama, must be carefully planned. There needs to be an adult involved in the project who is familiar with the restrictions of the elderly and what can and can't be done. While getting seniors up and moving is good for them, a doctor should review the plan to make sure that it is appropriate to the elderly people involved and won't cause any negative effects. Not only should this be the deciding factor as to whether a service-learning arts project is participatory or performance-based, but it should also influence just what seniors are being asked to do and how they do it.

With any project that involves elderly people, mental health plays a role as well. Many service-learning projects in the arts involve interaction between students and seniors, especially if they're working closely together on things like reminiscence or shared knowledge. Students should be aware of any danger signs that their elderly partner is not behaving normally, or perhaps is not feeling well on a particular day. Pay attention to signs like withdrawal, confusion, memory loss, or fatigue.

Although it is never the responsibility of a student to diagnose or cope with a mental health issue in his or her senior partner, it is possible for a teen to note changes in a partner and report them to the person in charge.

AND DON'T FORGET...

The arts don't just mean projects that involve performing arts. They can also include things like forming a student-senior book club, in which a student partners with an elderly person and they both read and then discuss a book. Book clubs can even be done on a whole classroom basis, and might culminate in a project in which seniors and students together write their own book or create a performance or artwork based on the book. It can also include writing, such as fiction or memoirs. Many elderly people have amazing life experiences and stories to share, which can be written down or even shared as oral history.

Overall, projects that involve collecting and sharing memories and reminiscences between students and seniors have their greatest value in allowing the elderly to interact in conversation with students. This is good for mental health because it provides seniors with the feeling that what they have to say is being heard and valued. And elderly people, especially those who live in residential centers apart from their relatives and community ties, appreciate the value of companionship and attention in a world that often seems to have set them aside and goes whizzing by without them.

Finally, other arts-related activities that make good service-learning projects involve elderly people sharing

When students and the elderly share stories, it fosters conversations and makes the older person feel valued and listened to.

their skills with students. This might include a craft such as embroidery, sewing, beading, or woodworking. It could also include, in a place that has the right facilities, things like baking and cooking. These projects often allow teens to be the recipients of knowledge from seniors, where they can learn a skill they didn't have before and their senior "teachers" can enjoy the feeling of having passed along a skill that they worked hard to achieve.

As with any service-learning project with the elderly, those involving the arts follow the same steps: investigate a need or an interest, plan a project to fit that need, take action to make the project take place, reflect on what has been learned, and then (especially easy for arts projects), plan a community celebration to show off the end result. Plays, concerts, art showings, and even meals and treats created through a project all make terrific sharing opportunities.

CHAPTER SIX

PARTNERS IN CARING

Service-learning projects with the elderly can be approached like any service-learning project, with a student or classroom researching a problem and creating a plan to address it. However, many projects seem to work best when done in partnership with a community group or an organization that specifically focuses on helping the elderly. These organizations often already have the structure in place for helping older people, making it easier and more efficient to make service-learning projects happen. And many of them welcome and even desperately need volunteers to help them with their mission.

SOMEONE IN THEIR CORNER

There are many national organizations that exist to advocate for the elderly. This means that their mission is to support the elderly by addressing issues important to them, such as Social Security, health care, and affordable housing. Some of these national groups are strong enough to lobby governments about legislation concerning senior issues. However, many of them also have branches on the state and local level and might be a good place to start looking for opportunities for service-learning projects or volunteering.

Some of the best-known organizations for elderly advocacy include the American Association of Retired Persons, the National Alliance for Caregiving, the National Center on Caregiving, the National Council on Aging, the National Family Caregivers Association, and the National Senior Citizens Law Center. These organizations can be resources for researching and choosing a service-learning need to address, and might be able to point the way to state or local organizations where volunteers and projects would be welcome. Communities often have organizations that exist to help families—including the elderly—and these can usually be found online or through local government. A school guidance counselor should also be able to help students find elderly advocacy groups in their own area.

Local churches often have existing groups or outreach programs for the elderly. Students who are involved in church-sponsored youth groups might find many opportunities for either volunteering or constructing service-learning projects through their churches. These can range from home visits to activities for seniors to organizing gift baskets or holiday items.

Students in a congregation may find that their place of worship is a great source for many service-learning opportunities with the elderly.

WHAT'S ALREADY THERE?

Another way to reach the elderly with service-learning volunteering has already been mentioned: partnering with a local nursing home or residential elderly housing community. These types of situations have a built-in population of older people who would enjoy, or perhaps even need, young volunteers and their service-learning projects.

Institutions that serve the elderly come in all different forms. At one end, there is a senior center or a recreational facility that holds programs for seniors. These generally serve elderly people who are still mobile and often still active and engaged in their community. They are more likely to need volunteers and services that are geared toward leisure activities or learning opportunities. Volunteering in a senior center might lead a teen to a service project of collecting oral histories, or sharing knowledge and learning from skills and abilities that seniors already have.

For active seniors, service-learning projects are more likely to be about leisure activities or learning opportunities, sometimes based on their skills and talents.

> ## WHAT'S
> ## THE DIFF?

Is there a difference between volunteering for an organization and doing a service-learning project with them? Yes. Ideally, a service-learning project not only addresses a need that the community already has—in this case, the elderly—but also links to the curriculum at a student's school. Service-learning projects are also generally thought up by, and put into action by, students together with their teachers. However, volunteering for an organization that supports the elderly might be a good framework for starting and carrying out a service-learning project because that organization is already established and has relationships with the elderly in the community.

Residential institutions for the elderly are next. They can range from communities that are specifically intended for retired people, where they still live independently, to facilities where the residents are less mobile and might have serious physical or mental health issues. Often they are limited as to what they can do. Volunteering at an institution such as this might involve performing tasks that have been determined by the institution, rather than creating new service projects. For example, student volunteers might read to residents, help with activities, distribute meals, or assist with moving residents from place to

Residents in elderly housing or hospital settings often need help with very basic activities, such as just moving from place to place.

place. However, even a stricter kind of volunteering can provide either ideas or opportunities for service-learning projects. If a student volunteer sees a need—such as a way to entertain residents beyond watching television, or to get them out of their chairs for mild exercise—then he or she can approach the institution's director about building a service-learning project.

Megan, whose grandfather is in a nursing home, was motivated to volunteer there after seeing what it was like. She wrote about her experiences on the *Teen Ink* website:

> I have painted the women's nails and read them letters from their children. I also have taken patients for walks. We also have birthday parties and exercise days. My volunteer experience has shown me that I can bring joy to older people. Everyone will have to face having parents and grandparents growing older and becoming dependent on their children. Dealing with this situation has made me a stronger and more caring person.

Hospitals might also have opportunities for student volunteers to work with the elderly, but because it is a hospital setting, this type of volunteering might not be limited just to elderly patients, and it will probably not have much scope for service-learning projects. Because the elderly in this setting are ill or injured, volunteering might be limited to simply providing companionship, distributing reading materials or flowers, or other small tasks.

> STEREOTYPES

When teens and the elderly interact through service-learning projects, one of the first things they might have to overcome are their stereotypes about each other. In the PBS show *Bridging the Gap*, students and seniors who interacted at a senior center during a service-learning project were asked the following questions about overcoming these stereotypical ideas about each other:

What kind of stereotypes might teens have about seniors that were dispelled in this program? Here are a few:

If seniors have physical difficulties, they aren't smart and creative. Seniors cannot relate to teens. Seniors might try to give advice without understanding a teen's situation or they might not have anything to talk about that would interest teens. Seniors are boring.

What kind of stereotypes do seniors have about teens that were dispelled? Here are a few:

Teens don't listen. Teens are not patient and move too fast. Teens cannot relate to older adults. Teens might not be polite. Teens want instant gratification and would not be interested in a project that takes a long time to complete.

BUT REMEMBER...

If students choose to do their service learning through partnerships with groups dedicated to the elderly, or establish projects through volunteering, there are probably strict rules and guidelines that volunteers must follow to work in the facility or institution. These rules are in place to protect both the elderly clients and the student volunteers. They might range from appropriate dress, to conduct, and to use of technology (cell phones and MP3 players, for example) while on the job. It is important to follow any rules so as to establish trust and create a good working relationship with both the group leaders and the elderly they serve.

If approaching service learning through a partnership or volunteer opportunity appeals to students, they can check with the service-learning coordinator or guidance counselor in their school for help in finding an appropriate place. They might find that spending some time among the elderly will inspire them with an idea for a service-learning project beyond the borders of their volunteer activities.

CHAPTER SEVEN

REAPING THE REWARDS

It's true that many teens perform service-learning projects because they either have to, as a requirement for a class, or because they need something that will look good on college applications or résumés. But service learning doesn't have to be just about earning a class credit or beefing up an application. Service-learning projects can be rewarding in other ways, too.

A group of teens involved in a 4H service-learning project in California was asked about the payoff for their work: "Teens …reported significant personal growth, changes in their perceptions, a sense of efficacy, and skill development. Teens (94 percent) felt as though they had made an important contribution to their community. Through the service-learning experience, they said they gained valuable skills including teamwork, communication and planning." Teens gain these skills from service learning, and they benefit from working closely with the elderly, who are themselves a huge resource of experience and skill. And for many teens, who might no longer have grandparents or might not be in contact with them, building these kinds of relationships can be incredibly rewarding and meaningful. Projects with the elderly are often a two-way street: Teens might provide projects that enhance the quality of life of seniors, but those same seniors might share experience, insights, affection, and even useful connections for the teen to use in his or her own life.

According to the HandsOn Network, service learning benefits teens in many ways:

Service learning doesn't just benefit the people who are being helped. It also benefits those who do the helping.

- Service learning can enhance personal development in areas such as self-esteem, moral reasoning, social skills, communication skills, problem-solving abilities, and concern for others and society.
- Involvement in service learning makes the subject matter in school real and relevant for students as they try out their knowledge and skills.

> A PATH TO A CAREER

Another benefit of service learning can be the opportunity to identify an interest that could lead to a future career. Teens with limited contact with the elderly might never know that they actually like older people and have a talent for getting along with them. A successful service-learning project, such as interacting with seniors, planning activities for them, or creating exercise and dance programs to help them move, might lead a teen to a human services career, such as physical therapy, dance, and music therapy, or being a residential or activities director for a senior center or nursing home. Many teens later realize that a service-learning project they performed in high school actually laid the groundwork for their future career path. In some cases, a teen might be able to create a relationship with an institution or facility that he or she can use for a formal job in the future.

If a teen participates in a service-learning project with the elderly and discovers a potential career path as a result, what's the next step? Obviously, she can continue to volunteer at a facility for the elderly, where she will gain more hands-on experience. But if her school has a vocational-technical center or department, she might be able to start taking classes while still in high school. Taking classes will help her find employment in human services jobs with the elderly. Check with the school guidance counselor to see what options are available for a head start on a career.

- When young people serve others, they can see that they are valued and can make a real difference.
- Young people learn leadership skills as they take responsibility for designing and implementing service experiences.

Service learning benefits everyone involved, from the student to the community. Organizations in particular gain because teens bring vitality and excitement to projects, they give the organization a higher profile through their school, and a new generation of volunteers is nurtured for the future.

WHAT DID I GAIN FROM SERVICE LEARNING WITH THE ELDERLY?

Whether a teen participates in service learning for classroom credit or college applications, at the end of the day, the rewards of a project with the elderly are many and go far beyond simply getting a good grade or getting into college. In an article on the influence of service learning on teens' attitudes toward

Service-learning projects are more than just a means to a good grade; they are often very rewarding for everyone involved, no matter what their role.

> **CLOSE TO HOME**

Service learning not only benefits teens by creating relationships with the elderly in their communities. It can also help them with their own elderly family members. In Norma Nealeigh's "Bridging the Gaps: A Service-Learning Project," one service-learning participant explained how it completely changed a relationship in her own family: "My grandmother and I have never gotten along. She thought I was a young rebellious brat, and I always thought she was an old fuddy-duddy. Since getting to know my senior partner and understanding her life experiences, I have begun to see my grandmother in a new way, and we are actually talking now."

older people, K. Dale Layfield asked teens what they learned from their experiences:

"Working with my person, I have learned how not to judge people before you really know who they are. I have learned not to classify people and just put them into groups without giving them a chance."

"I found out how much the older people know and how much I can learn from them. My person

A school service-learning project can result in new relationships between students, the elderly, and their own family members.

has traveled all over the world. She really wants to learn from us and is really interested in sharing with us and is interested in our lives and what we have to teach her."

Hopefully this is what teens will remember from their service-learning projects with the elderly, long after they have graduated from high school and college. Service learning will benefit everyone involved, from those helping, to those being helped, to the wider community, and even the world. As the anthropologist Margaret Mead said, "Never doubt that a small group of thoughtful, committed citizens can change the world. Indeed, it's the only thing that ever has."

GLOSSARY

administrative Related to running a business or organization.

advocate To publicly recommend or support a cause or policy.

assessment The evaluation of the nature, quality, or ability of someone or something.

client A person who uses the services of a professional or company.

curriculum The subjects that make up the course of study in school or college.

dehydration The state of suffering from a lack of water.

dementia A mental disorder marked by memory disorders, personality changes, and impaired reasoning.

hospice An organization or home that provides care for the sick, especially the terminally ill.

implementation The practice of putting a decision, plan, or agreement into effect.

integral Essential or necessary to make something complete.

languish To lose or lack vitality; to grow weak or feeble.

malnutrition Not having enough to eat, or not eating enough of the right things.

memorabilia Objects collected or saved because of their personal or historical interest.

mobility The ability to move freely and easily.

refurbish To renovate, repair, or redecorate something.

savvy Shrewd or knowledgeable about the realities of life or certain subjects.

therapy Treatment intended to relieve or heal a disorder.

vocational Relating to an occupation or job.

Canadian Alliance for Community Service-Learning
2128 Dunton Tower
Carleton University
1125 Colonel By Drive
Ottawa, ON, K1S 5B6
Canada
(613) 520-2600 Ext 82
E-mail: info@communityservicelearning.ca
Website: http://www.communityservicelearning.ca/
    en/welcome_what_is.htm
This organization supports the growth of community
    service-learning in Canada, with students, educators
    and communities learning and working together to
    strengthen individuals and society.

Canadian Community Economic Development Network
59, rue Monfette, P.O. Box 119E
Victoriaville, QC G6P 1J8
Canada
(877) 202-2268
E-mail: info@ccednet-rcdec.ca
Website: https://ccednet-rcdec.ca/en
This community development organization supports and
    fosters service-learning opportunities in Canadian
    communities. It explores ways that learning in the
    community contributes to the development of citizen-
    ship and increases the capacity to affect social and
    economic change.

Institute for Global Education and Service-Learning
55 Handy Road

Levittown, PA 19056
(267) 235-4974
E-mail: institute@igesl.org
Website: http://igesl.org
The Institute for Global Education and Service-Learning is a nonprofit training organization that creates service-learning programs and activity-based education in collaboration with schools and organizations around the world.

International Association for Research on Service-Learning and Community Engagement
Tulane University Center for Public Service
Alcee Fortier Hall
6823 St. Charles Avenue
New Orleans, LA 70118
(504) 862-3366
Website: http://www.researchslce.org
This organization promotes research into service learning in all levels of education to advance knowledge of service learning and community service.

National Society for Experiential Education (NSEE)
c/o Talley Management Group, Inc.
19 Mantua Road
Mt. Royal, NJ 08061
(856) 423-3427
E-mail: nsee@talley.com
Website: http://www.nsee.org
This nonprofit group of educators and business and community leaders develops and promotes

opportunities for service learning. It also sponsors workshops, volunteer opportunities, and professional development for educators.

National Youth Leadership Council
1667 Snelling Avenue North, Suite D300
Saint Paul, MN 55108
(651) 631-3672
Website: http://www.nylc.org
This group provides programs and services that advance the field of service learning as well as encouraging youth leadership and supporting educators.

WEBSITES

Because of the changing nature of Internet links, Rosen Publishing has developed an online list of websites related to the subject of this book. This site is updated regularly. Please use this link to access the list:

http://www.rosenlinks.com/SLFT/Elder

FOR FURTHER READING

Bordessa, Chris. *Team Challenges: 170+ Group Activities to Build Cooperation, Communication, and Creativity.* Chicago, IL: Chicago Review Press, 2012.

Cipolle, Susan Benigni. *Service-Learning and Social Justice: Engaging Students in Social Change.* Lanham, MD: Rowman & Littlefield, 2010.

Cress, Christine M. *Learning Through Serving: A Student Guidebook for Service-Learning and Civic Engagement Across Academic Disciplines and Cultural Communities.* 2nd ed. Sterling, VA: Stylus Publishing, 2013.

Dolgon, Carey W., and Christopher W. Baker. *Social Problems: A Service Learning Approach.* Thousand Oaks, CA: Sage Publications, 2010.

Duncan, Dawn, and Joan Kopperud. *Service-Learning Companion.* Farmington Hills, MI: Cengage, 2008.

Engdahl, Sylvia. *The Elderly* (Current Controversies). Farmington Hills, MI: Greenhaven Press, 2011.

Farber, Katy. *Change the World with Service Learning: How to Create, Lead, and Assess Service Learning Projects.* Lanham, MD: R&L Education, 2011.

Frankfort, Lisa, Matthew McKay, and Peter Rogers. *The Community Building Companion: 50 Ways to Make Connections and Create Change in Your Own Backyard.* Oakland, CA: New Harbinger Publications, 2002.

Friedman, Jenny. *The Busy Family's Guide to Volunteering: Do Good, Have Fun, Make a Difference as a Family!* Lewisville, NC: Gryphon House, 2003.

Friedman, Jenny. *Doing Good Together: 101 Easy, Meaningful Service Projects for Families, Schools,* and Communities. Minneapolis, MN: Free Spirit Publishing, 2010.

Gay, Kathlyn. Volunteering: The Ultimate Teen Guide (It Happened to Me). Lanham, MD: Scarecrow Press, 2007.

Grabinski, C. Joanne. 101 Careers in Gerontology. New York, NY: Springer Publishing, 2007.

Joos, Kristin E. Don't Just Count Your Hours, Make Your Hours Count: The Essential Guide to Volunteering & Community Service. Lakeland, FL: Treetop Software Company, 2011.

Kaye, Cathryn Berger. The Complete Guide to Service Learning: Proven, Practical Ways to Engage Students in Civic Responsibility, Academic Curriculum, & Social Action. Minneapolis, MN: Free Spirit Publishing, 2010.

KIDS Consortium. Integrating Scientific Practices and Service-Learning: Engaging Students in STEM. Augurn, ME: KIDS Consortium, 2011.

KIDS Consortium. Kids as Planners: A Guide to Strengthening Students, Schools, and Communities Through Service-Learning. 3rd ed. Augurn, ME: KIDS Consortium, 2011.

KIDS Consortium. Working with KIDS: A Service-Learning Guide for Community Partners. Augurn, ME: KIDS Consortium, 2011.

Kronick, Robert F., Robert B. Cunningham, and Michele Gourley. Experiencing Service-Learning. Knoxville, TN: University of Tennessee Press, 2011.

LeMay, Kathy. The Generosity Plan: Sharing Your Time, Treasure, and Talent to Shape the World. New York, NY: Atria Books, 2010.

Lewis, Barbara A. *The Kid's Guide to Service Projects: Over 500 Service Ideas for Young People Who Want to Make a Difference.* Minneapolis, MN: Free Spirit Publishing, 2009.

Lewis, Barbara A. *The Teen Guide to Global Action: How to Connect with Others (Near & Far) to Create Social Change.* Minneapolis, MN: Free Spirit Publishing, 2007.

Murphy, Timothy, and Jon Tan, eds. *Service-Learning and Educating in Challenging Contexts: International Perspectives.* New York, NY: Bloomsbury Academic, 2012.

Robinson, Jerry W., and Gary P. Green. *Introduction to Community Development: Theory, Practice, and Service-Learning.* Thousand Oaks, CA: Sage Publications, 2010.

Stoecker, Randy. *The Unheard Voices: Community Organizations and Service Learning.* Philadelphia, PA: Temple University Press, 2009.

Sundem, Garth. *Real Kids, Real Stories, Real Change: Courageous Actions Around the World.* Minneapolis, MN: Free Spirit Publishing, 2010.

BIBLIOGRAPHY

Angres, Rachel. "The New Pervasive Culture of Civic Engagement." Youtopia, February 12, 2013. Retrieved February 12, 2014 (http://www.youtopia.com/info/the-new-culture-civics).

Arizona Attorney General Tom Horne. "Elder Abuse Information and Training Guide." Retrieved February 15, 2014 (https://www.azag.gov/seniors/elder-abuse-information-and-training-guide#5).

Boutwell, Ashley, teenage service-learning volunteer. Interview with the author. March 6, 2014.

Clemente, Joanne. "In the Mix: Bridging the Years… Teens and Seniors Mix It Up!" PBS, 2009. Retrieved February 12, 2014 (http://www-tc.pbs.org/inthemix/educators/lessons/bridgingtheyears_guide.pdf).

Creativity Matters: The Arts and Aging Toolkit. "Chapter 1: Understanding the Context for Arts and Aging Programs." Retrieved February 16, 2014 (http://artsandaging.org/index.php?id=1).

Esikoff, Alexei, Susan Ragsdale, and Nancy Tuminelly. "Engaging Teens with Their Community: A Service Learning Resource." YMCA of the USA, 2008. Retrieved February 16, 2014 (http://www.ymca.net/sites/default/files/service-learning-resources/service-learning-resource.pdf).

Farber, Katy. Change the World with Service Learning: How to Organize, Lead, and Assess Service Learning Projects. Lanham, MD: Rowman & Littlefield Education, 2011.

HandsOn Network. "18 Benefits of Service Learning." August 23, 2013. Retrieved February 13, 2014 (http://handsonblog.org/2011/08/23/18-benefits-of-service-learning).

Institute for Intercultural Studies. "Frequently Asked Questions About Mead/Bateson." Retrieved March 2, 2014 (http://www.interculturalstudies.org/faq .html#quote).

Knight-Ridder Newspapers. "Teen-ager Teaches Martial Arts to Seniors." *Amarillo Globe-News*, September 29, 2002. Retrieved February 16, 2014 (http:// amarillo.com/stories/2002/10/01/new_ teenagersteaches.html).

Langley, Liz, teenage service-learning volunteer. Interview with the author. March 6, 2014.

Layfield, K. Dale. "Impact of Intergenerational Service Learning on Students' Stereotypes Toward Older People in an Introductory Agricultural Computing Course." *Journal of Southern Agricultural Education Research*, Vol. 54, No. 1, 2004. Retrieved February 14, 2014 (http://www.jsaer.org/pdf/Vol54/54-01-134.pdf).

Levinson, Matt. "Service Learning and Technology: Linking Teens and the Elderly." From Fear to Facebook, August 27, 2010. Retrieved February 16, 2014 (http://fromfeartofacebook.com/2010/08/27/ service-learning-and-technology-linking-teens-and -the-elderly).

Lewis, Barbara A. *The Kid's Guide to Service Projects: Over 500 Service Ideas for Young People Who Want to Make a Difference*. Minneapolis, MN: Free Spirit Publishing, 2009.

National Center for Education Statistics. "K-12 Public Schools," 1999. Retrieved February 14, 2014 (http://nces.ed.gov/pubs99/1999043.pdf).

National Commission on Service-Learning. "Learning in Deed: The Power of Service-Learning for

American Schools." Retrieved February 14, 2014 (http://www.cpn.org/topics/youth/k12/pdfs/Learning_in_Deed.pdf).

Nealeigh, Norma. "Bridging the Gaps: A Service-Learning Project." Human Sciences Honor Society: Kappa Omicron Nu. Retrieved March 2, 2014 (http://www.kon.org/archives/forum/15-2/nealeigh.htm).

P., Megan "Helping the Elderly: My Volunteer Experiences." *Teen Ink*. Retrieved February 15, 2014 (http://www.teenink.com/hot_topics/community_service/article/4023/Helping-The-Elderly-My-Volunteer-Experiences).

Pew Research Center. "Attitudes About Aging: A Global Perspective: Chapter 2. Aging in the U.S. and Other Countries, 2010 to 2050." Pew Research Global Attitudes Project, January 30, 2014. Retrieved February 13, 2014 (http://www.pewglobal.org/2014/01/30/chapter-2-aging-in-the-u-s-and-other-countries-2010-to-2050).

Shellenbarger, Sue. "Teens Teach Tech to Seniors." *Wall Street Journal: The Juggle*, January 11, 2011. Retrieved February 13, 2014 (http://blogs.wsj.com/juggle/2011/01/11/teens-teach-tech-to-seniors).

Spring, Kimberly, Robert Grimm Jr., and Nathan Dietz. "Community Service and Service-Learning in America's Schools." Corporation for National and Community Service, 2008. Retrieved February 15, 2014 (http://www.nationalservice.gov/pdf/08_1112_lsa_prevalence.pdf).

Stevenson, Sarah. "10 Symptoms of Mental Illness in the Elderly." *A Place for Mom*, October 7, 2013. Retrieved February 15, 2014 (http://www.aplaceformom.com/blog/2013-10-7-mental-illness-in-the-elderly).

University of California. "Service-Learning Works for California 4-H Youth." University of California 4-H Youth Development Program. Retrieved February 25, 2014 (http://4h.ucanr.edu/News/Impacts/?impact=672&a=2071).

V., Diolinda. "Helping the Elderly." *Teen Ink*. Retrieved February 15, 2014 (http://www.teenink.com/hot_topics/community_service/article/4067/Helping-The-Elderly).

INDEX

ABOUT THE AUTHOR

Marcia Amidon Lusted has written 90 books and more than 450 articles for young readers. She is also an associate editor and staff writer for Cobblestone Publishing's six magazines. She has participated in many community service projects with the elderly, and frequently sees firsthand what their needs are and how they benefit from students performing service-learning projects with them.

PHOTO CREDITS